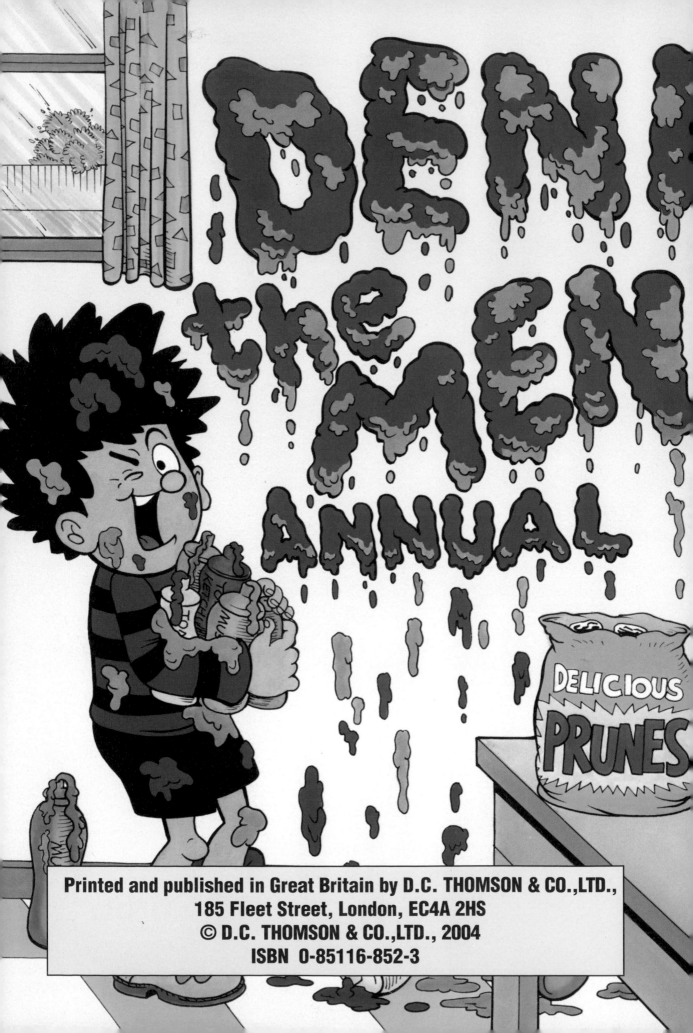

Printed and published in Great Britain by D.C. THOMSON & CO.,LTD.,
185 Fleet Street, London, EC4A 2HS
© D.C. THOMSON & CO.,LTD., 2004
ISBN 0-85116-852-3

DENNiS the MENACE and friends

Uh? What's the white stuff in Dennis's hair?

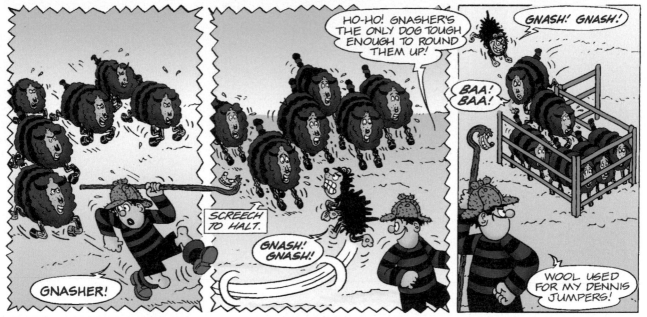

GNASHER!

SCREECH TO HALT.

GNASH! GNASH!

HO-HO! GNASHER'S THE ONLY DOG TOUGH ENOUGH TO ROUND THEM UP!

GNASH! GNASH!

BAA! BAA!

WOOL USED FOR MY DENNIS JUMPERS!

GNASHER ALSO COLLECTS THE COATS!

CLICK!

SHRIEK!

GNASH!

EEK!

HAR-HAR! THEY'VE LEAPT OUT OF THEIR COATS!

AND—

GREAT! ENOUGH FOR QUITE A FEW JUMPERS HERE!

GNASH!

GRAB

BUT—

CHEEP-HEE! CHORTLE! HMM! HOLD ON!

SHIVER

HEH! HEH!

LATER—

HAR-HAR! KEEP MY SPARE JUMPERS TILL YOUR COATS GROW BACK!

BAA-OK!

BAA!

BAA-HAH!

The Menacing

CANADA

IRELAND

RODEO RIDING

AMERICA

AMERICAN
FOOTBALL

BARRY GLENNARD

YOU'RE LOOKING FIT! HOW'S YOUR EYESIGHT, GRANNY?

HUH! I CAN STILL...

BOP!

TWANG!

...KNOCK OFF A POLICEMAN'S HELMET AT A HUNDRED PACES...

...AND OUTRUN HIM TOO! CHORTLE!

C'MERE, YOU OLD-AGED PEST!

IN THE PARK—

KNITTING SOCKS THESE DAYS?

CLICK! CLICK!

NO— ROPE-LADDERS FOR CLIMBING TREES! HAR-HAR!

EH?

THROW

PELT THE SOFTIES!

SOFT GRASS FOR PICNICS

OO!

SPLAT!

HANDY HAVING ROTTEN FRUIT IN YOUR HANDBAG!

YELP!

YAHOO!

SLIDE

TEA TIME! LET'S GO HOME, GRANNY!

BACK HOME—

TO YOUR ROOM, DENNIS! YOU TOO, GRANNY!

THAT'S THE BAND OF MENACES!

HUH! SENT TO MY ROOM! MENACING FUN'S OVER FOR TODAY, GRANNY!

CLICK! CLICK!

DENNIS'S BEDROOM

EH?

WAHEY! THAT'S WHAT YOU THINK, DENNIS!

CLICK!

WAH!

THROB

BLOW!

RAT-TAT-TAT!

HAR-HAR! GRANNY'S UMBRELLA'S A LONG-RANGE PEA-SHOOTER!

OUCH!

OW!

GNASH!

PEAS

GNAHA!

DASH

COME AND HEAR IRIS PANSY DISCUSS FLOWER ARRANGING

I GNOW WHERE TO GET SPEAKERS!

ZOOM

I'D LIKE TO SPEAK TO YOU ALL ABOUT GERANIUMS. AND GLADIOLI!

THUD! THUD!

GOODY!

GOSH!

EEK! UNHAND ME AT ONCE!

STOP GNAGGING! C'MON. I GNOW ANOTHER PLACE TO FIND A SPEAKER.

At the Houses of Parliament —

MR SPEAKER! MR SPEAKER!

BEANO

TEE-HEE!

DOCTORS LINE

ORDER! ORDER! ORDER! ORDER!

THAT'S THE NEW SPEAKERS ORDERED.

GWAIT! I'VE FOUND TWO SPEAKERS FOR YOU!

SORRY, GNASHER! THEY'RE THE WRONG TYPES OF SPEAKERS. WE NEED SPEAKERS FOR A GIG WE'VE GOT COMING UP.

MUSIC SHOP

DENNIS AND THE DIN-MAKERS, THAT IS! AND YOU'RE OUR DRUMMER!

GNUH? GASP!

SCREECH TO HALT!

COME TO THE GIG, READERS. OVER THE PAGE.

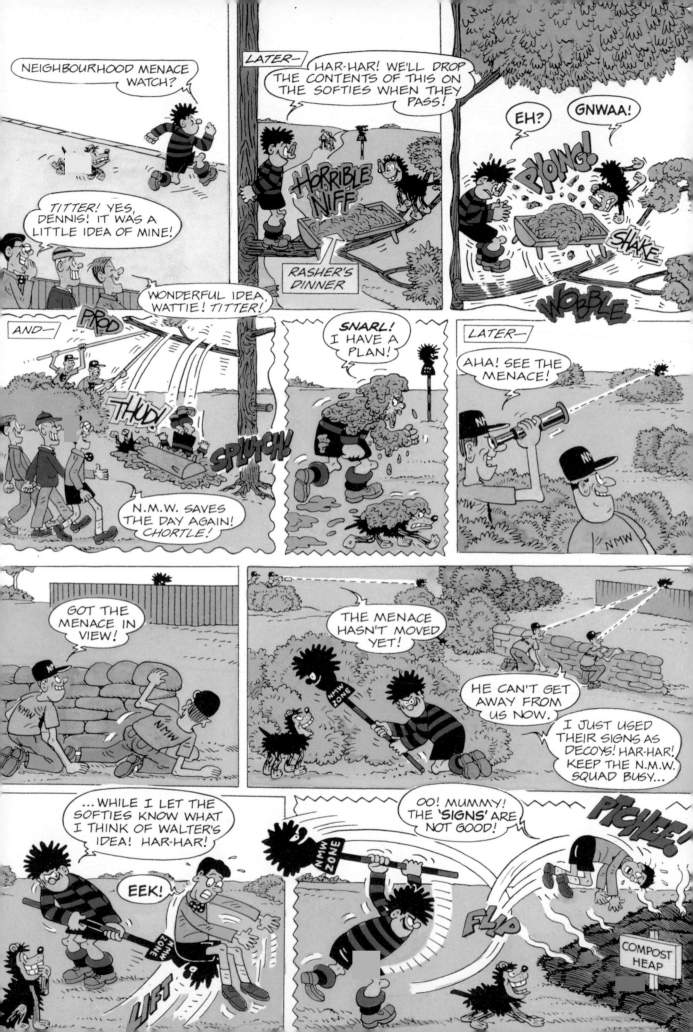

THE WORMS THAT TURNED !

THESE PANCAKES ARE SIMPLY SCRUMPTIOUS! YOU MUST GIVE ME THE RECIPE, WALTER, DEAR CHUM.

EH?

POUR

THEY SMELL BETTER THAN YOUR "PANCAKES"!

OH, WAIT! THIS ISN'T A TRACK ON THE MAP.

IT'S A BIT OF SPAGHETTI! SLURP!

OO!

WAFT!

GSORRY 'BOUT THAT, I ATE TOO MANY PANCAKES!

I PLANT THIS FLAG TO CLAIM THIS HILL FOR MENACEDOM!

OH, YEAH?

MENACES FOREVER

Don't BE A GOOD SPORT

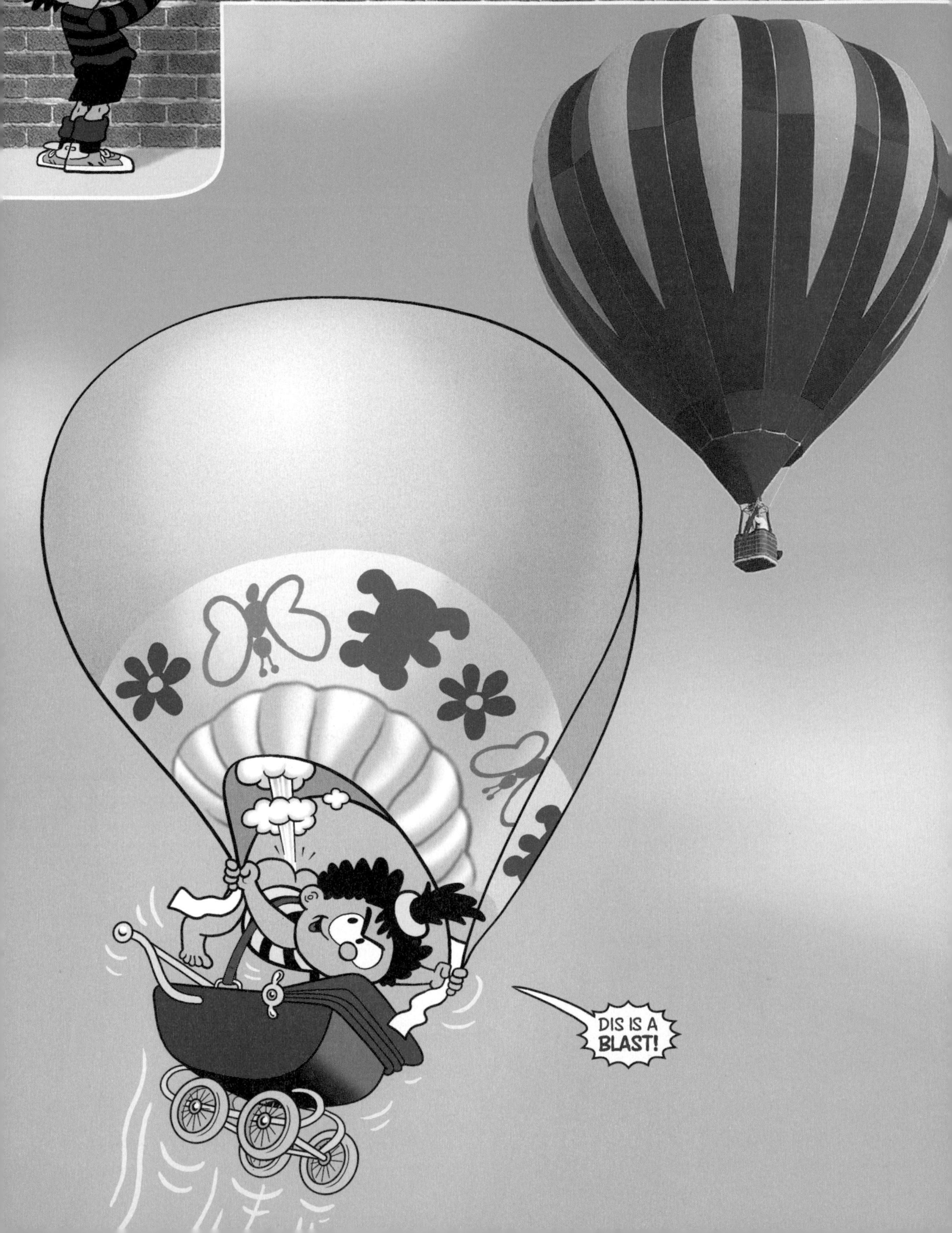

HOW DOES YOUR GARDEN GROO?

YES, MY LITTLE WALTER HAS SUCH GREEN FINGERS! SO TALENTED A GARDENER!

TUM-TI-TUM!

BAH! SWOT!

DENNIS'S ROCKERY

HEY! WE'VE GOT GREEN FINGERS, TOO!

YER! 'AT'S RIGHT!

ER, NO! NOT THAT KIND OF GREEN FINGERS, BEA!

EH?

QUICK! TURN THE PAGE, READERS, TO SEE THE PLANTS A MENACE SHOULD GROW!

AW! ME'S GOT A LUMPY ONE UP THERE!

GOUGE

SCHOOL FOR MENACES

AFTER YOU!

NO, NO—AFTER YOU, SIR!

I'LL CARRY YOUR BAG!

AND I'LL HELP YOU ACROSS THE STREET!

YOU'RE LOOKING VERY WELL!

GOOD DAY! ALL THE BETTER FOR SEEING YOU!

HUH! BEANOTOWN'S TOO NICE A PLACE THESE DAYS. WE NEED MORE MENACES ON THE STREETS! I'LL FIX IT, GNASHER!

BECOME A FULLY QUALIFIED MENACE!

ONE BEANO PER LESSON

CUSTARD PIE RANGE

TAKE THAT!

SPLAT!

SPLAT!

SPLAT!

HEH-HEH!

BEANOS HERE

1000 RASPS—THEN MOVE ON!

RAZZ!

THIS LOOKS GREAT FUN!

KEEP UP THE GOOD WORK! HAR-HAR-HAR!

PEA SHOOTER TARGET

PING!

PING!

MENACES TRAINING CAMP

PEA SHOOTER

PEAS

4. . . . but Dennis had always maintained Gansher should have lots of iron in his diet, so that was okay!

6. . . . so Dennis had the race IN THE BAG!

PIGS WILL!

LET'S GO AND FETCH MY PET PORKER, RASHER. HE LOVES TO GO MENACING!

GNASH! GNASH!

BUT—

PHEW! NO SIGN OF RASHER AND A DAY'S SWILL LEFT UNTOUCHED! VERY ODD!

RASHER

THEN—

SPLOSH!

DRIP DRIP

WOW! GASP! MY RASHER! HAS HE CAUGHT RAVING LOONEY PIG DISEASE?

SCRUB

PIGGY CREAM

GRUNTY... GRUNT...

TURNIP SCENTED SHOWER GEL

GNEH?

SWING WHEN YOU'RE WINNING

MY NEIGHBOUR, THE WORLD FAMOUS EXPLORER STANLEY LIVINGSTONE, HAS RETURNED FROM A TRIP. I'M GOING TO VISIT HIM!

IN STAN'S HOUSE.

THIS IS A GREAT WAY OF STAYING OUT OF TROUBLE IN THE JUNGLE, DENNIS!

SWING

HMM! STAYING OUT OF TROUBLE, EH?

SO—

HAR-HAR! SWINGING ALONG CAN KEEP ME OUT OF TROUBLE TOO!

A LOAF BAKER

GRAB

SOOT BOMBS

GRR! IT'S DENNIS!

SPLAT

LADIES Fashion

SPLAT

AAGH! THE MENACE!

OOF!

SUPER SALE TODAY

HUMPH! END OF SIGNS....

....NOT END OF MY, SWINGING, THOUGH! WHEEE!

ER LE DAY

DING DONG BING BONG

GRAB

SWING

EH?

ERK?

I'M NOT FINISHED YET! I'LL NEED YOUR HELP, GNASHER!

OO-YAH!

EEK!

WE'LL NEED EXTRA LENGTH IF WE'RE TO CATCH THE NEXT ROPE! GO FOR IT, GNASHER!

GNASH! GNASH!

ZOOM

HE'S GOT IT!

BITE

ULP! I FORGOT—GNASHER'S TEETH CAN BITE THROUGH STEEL WIRE!

SNIP

TUMBLE

HEH-HEH!

THUD

BOOMF

MEANWHILE AND THEN IN THE JUNGLE WE HEARD STRANGE NOISES.......

SLOO!

BOOM! BANGA! BOOM-BOOM-THUD!

WAIT! A MESSAGE ON JUNGLE DRUMS! I CAN TRANSLATE FOR YOU! AH......YES...

ER....DRUMS SAY-'ONE-EYED CHICKEN IS DANCING ON A POLICEMAN'S HEAD'! VERY ODD!

I THINK I CAN TRANSLATE THAT MESSAGE TO MAKE MORE SENSE!

SO–

LOTS OF COMPLAINTS ABOUT DENNIS AT OUR DOOR!

GRRR!

PSSST! KEEP QUIET, GNASHER!

BOOM BANGA

BOOM

THUD

Don't BE A GOOD SPORT

DENNIS THE MENACE IN... 'SO LOW POLO'

I'M OFF TO PLAY POLO, PALS!

QUITE! POLO! SOOPER GAME, IS IT NOT? YOU GET TO WEAR ALL THE LATEST FASHIONS, DOESN'T ONE KNOW?

← STIFLED CHUCKLE

SNIGGER! LOOK AT WALTER! WHAT A WET WALLY!

AND YOU MEET SUCH SPIFFING FELLOWS! THESE ARE MY NEW CHUMS.

HOORAH! I'M TARQUIN.

I'M JUSTIN.

AND I'M JULIAN.

COR! A SOFTY SELECTION!

GLIDE TO HALT!

NO WONDER THEY ALL PLAY POLO — THEY LOOK LIKE HORSES THEMSELVES!!!

BUT YOU CAN'T PLAY POLO, MENACE! IT'S A GAME FOR US POSH PEOPLE.

MORE THAN ONE KIND OF POLO!

SO I WAS WRONG. THERE ARE MORE THAN **TWO** KINDS OF POLO!

DAB

At the polo ground —

I SAY! SHOULDN'T WE PLAY A GAME?

NO WAY, JULIAN! THOSE HORSES SMELL! AND I DON'T WANT TO DIRTY MY NEW SILK SHIRT.

THOSE SADDLES! SO UNCOMFORTABLE ON ONE'S BEAM END!

ELEPHANT POLO! THAT'S THE OTHER KIND. IT'S ALL THE RAGE IN ASIA!

WANT TO PLAY?

EEK!

THAT'S HANDY! WALTER IS FROZEN STIFF WITH FEAR!

FROZEN STIFF WITH FEAR

SWISH SWISH

TIME WE GOT OUT OF HERE!

TOO TRUE, TARQUIN!

I'LL NEVER CATCH THEM. HOWEVER, I DO HAVE SOME PEPPER.

SHAKE

PEPPER

SNUFFLE

FLEE, FRIENDS!

TA!

No, but the elephant's sneeze might. Wait for it, Readers . . .

WHEEEEE

SPEED—SEVERAL HUNDRED MILES AN HOUR!

WELL, ELEPHANT POLO IS GREAT FUN. BUT THERE'S ONE BIG PROBLEM.

EVEN ME FINKS 'AT STINKS!

SHOVE

Don't
BE A GOOD SPORT
TUT-TUT-TUT! GRASS STAINS ARE SO HARD TO GET OUT!
Sudso